Herobrine Rise Of The Sa

By Barry J McDonald

www.MinecraftNovels.com

Chapter 1

"You wouldn't think it to look at me but I was there that day," the witch said gazing off into space. "Well, I was a lot younger then. Back then my youngest sister and I used to love playing hide and seek, climbing trees and exploring caves. We did all the things young kids love doing and aren't supposed to do. Then - he came. He looked different from us. Of course we all thought that he was part of the game but that didn't last long." Herobrine nodded.

"We watched him from up on a hill, my sister and I. She was the curious one but I warned her. I told her not to get close, but she wouldn't listen. She was only five, and he cut her down like an animal. I'll never get that scene out of my mind," the witch said and sighed.

"You think we're the monsters in this world Herobrine. Think again. The world before mightn't have been perfect, but it was a lot better than this. We took what we needed, and that was it. We all got along together," the witch said and paused as Herobrine scratched on the ground with his sword.

"Hostile mobs, they weren't around then," the witch said and cackled. "We'd no reason for them. No, they came because of the outsiders." The witch smiled at the confused look on Herobrine's face. "It's funny for a man who can control hostile mobs at will, that you don't know much about them."

Taking out a pork chop, the witch tore off a part and started to chew on it. Waiting until she'd finished, she then continued.

"As I said it was because of them that the hostile mobs came into being. I'll never forget that day going home to my parents and telling them what had happened to my sister. As you can imagine, they were devastated. In a few more days we found out we weren't the only ones to suffer from the players. Word got around that the outsiders were taking over mines, killing villagers and animals for sport. They couldn't be allowed to do whatever they wanted any more. It was decided that we'd get revenge for what they were doing. All the witches and those who practiced magic all got together and used their powers to create hostile mobs. That worked for a while but unfortunately they too started to be killed. The players had found out how to create better weapons with stronger metals. Then they discovered our flaws and limitations and used them to their advantage. It looked like they could never be beaten. Then, you came." Herobrine raised his eyebrows and pointed at himself.

"Yes, you. As I said before, my eldest sister was an idiot. But maybe a genius at the same time. Who knew that a player from the other side would be a hero for us here? You're the only one that has the benefits of both worlds. You've got skill with a sword and you've got control of the hostile mobs. That's what has them scared."

Herobrine thought over what the witch had said and had to agree she did have a point. He'd never thought about it before. He was indeed a mixture of both worlds, but he was also a mixture of the good and the bad. This had left him being hated by both sides and wanted dead by all. Something that he wondered if he'd ever be able to break free from.

"Never thought about it? You can see what I'm saying is true. And it's because of you that they're scared," the witch said. "If they could get you out of the game they'd be free to do whatever they wanted. You know how that would end, don't you? You remember how those players griefed off you and killed your friend and dog. Would you like to see that done to other new players, bullied and robbed? No, they can't be allowed to get control of Minecraft. That's where you come in."

As he listened, Herobrine knew that the witch was turning the story to suit herself but there was also a grain of truth in there. Players having the freedom of Minecraft mightn't be a good idea. With no one to police them, he could see how things could get out of control. He knew that most players were good and just wanted to have fun, but there were always a few rotten apples that would spoil it.

"Well, ready to have some fun? I haven't told you why we're here. You see that hill over there," the witch said pointing into the distance. "Behind it are a group of players who call themselves the Samurai. These Samurai, have started to offer protection from us. I have to admit they're good, better than most players here. Now players from all over are queuing up to pay them protection money. If it was one or two groups that would be OK, but now they've started to spring up all over Minecraft. That's where you come in." Herobrine knew what was coming next.

"You're going to break this group wide open. They can't be allowed to continue doing this. We can't allow players to take control of… our world. It was ours before and it will be ours again. They're going to learn what it's like to mess with us!" the witch said with a grin.

Chapter 2

Looking in the direction that these samurai were supposed to be in, Herobrine played over in his mind what the witch had said. He could understand why she was doing it, but what was the point. There was no way to stop the flood of players coming into Minecraft. Even if he did give the witches and hostile mobs the upper hand, it would only be for a short while. Things would just go back to what they were before. This plan wasn't going to work. Taking out his sword Herobrine wrote on the ground with its tip.

"Too late!" the witch said reading the words. "How? It's never too late. You heard me they're taking over this place and doing what they want with it. Building stupid creations and robbing our world of its treasures. It can't continue. I know part of you agrees with me," the witch said rubbing out Herobrine's words with her foot. "No player can be allowed to get so big here that they can do whatever they want. You know where that leads don't you?"

Herobrine nodded his head. He knew only too well how some player's greed for money and power had ruined the game for others. He'd fought enough of them in his time. "I don't have to remind you of why you're doing this," the witch said and pulled a small potion bottle out of her pocket. "You don't do as I say, and well, you know what'll happen." Herobrine pointed his sword tip at the witch. There was no way he was going to let her take back the cure she'd given SparkleGirl.

"I thought we had an agreement?" the witch said

pretending to be hurt. "A quick teleport and I could be back there beside her. You know that don't you. Do you want me to do that, change her back to that monster she'd become?" Herobrine lowered his sword. He knew she'd do it in an instant without a thought.

Then without warning the witch threw the potion bottle to him. Stunned, he held it in his hand and looked at the liquid contents inside. "Wondering if it's the cure? It is. You're now holding what you want. Go, I can see that I'm wasting my time with you. I thought you were a clever man but I can see I was wrong. Don't say I didn't warn you when they come looking for you!" the witch said over her shoulder walking away.

Hearing what she'd said, Herobrine walked after her, grabbed her shoulder and spun her around. Staring at her with his white intense eyes he tried to read her face.

"Sorry, you didn't know. Yeah, they're looking for you too. You don't see yourself as being one, but you're a hostile mob too," the witch said with a grin. "Once they get a hold of this place, it'll only be a matter of time before they come looking for you. Then when you've no one like me, or your creepers to save the day, then what are you going to do? You mightn't like to think it but I'm a better friend than they are," the witch said pointing off in the direction of the samurai. "And then, there's SparkleGirl and Emman. They're targets too, you know that?"

Herobrine took a step backwards and thought over what she'd said. He hadn't thought of his friends as being enemies of the samurai, but he knew they would be. They could be used as hostages or worse killed because of him.

"Still want to go home and play happy families? You know

what I'm saying is true. If they're intent on wiping out all the hostile mobs, you're going to be on that list too," the witch said.

Herobrine wrote on the ground again with his sword. "How, how do I know all of this? Let's just say not all of us hostile mobs see it the same way as I do. They've got a witch working for them," the witch said and spat. "Imagine that. One of our own and they're working on our destruction. I don't know what they've promised her, but she's giving them weapons and potions and they're using them against us. We lost four yesterday, four witches died because of her. You might have time before they come looking for you, but for me, it's not very far away."

Herobrine scratched the ground again with his sword. "If you kill her, will that be enough?" the witch said. "I don't know but it'll definitely put their plans on the scrapheap for a while. Maybe once they've lost their supply it might make them more vulnerable to attack. Then maybe we might be able to put up a better fight. That is unless she did the other thing..."

Herobrine didn't like it when the witch paused like that. She'd already told him a few things he didn't want to hear, so this pause didn't sound like good news was on the way.

"I don't know how to say this but..." the witch paused. "But I think they've made another version of you."

Chapter 3

Herobrine went to the closest rock and sat on it. His mind was reeling at the witch's last comment. Someone like him. It wasn't worth thinking about. He knew the destruction he had caused in his earlier days, now the thought that someone else would also have that power. It was madness.

"We might have time," the witch said sitting down beside him. "I'd heard that she'd been working on this idea for a while now, but I don't know if she completed it. The sooner we act the better. Then maybe we can get to her before she does the unthinkable."

Holding the potion bottle in his hand Herobrine looked at it. He'd thought that getting this would be the answer to his prayers and he would finally live a life in peace. But like the potion inside, he too was trapped. Trapped and unable to get away.

"She means a lot to you, doesn't she? I wasn't going to use it on her. I knew if I had to keep the threat of using the potion as a way of controlling you, I knew you'd find a way out of helping me. But if I could get you here and tell you why I needed you, then maybe you'd stay of your own free will," the witch said. "We may have been enemies in the past, but right now I could be the best friend you ever had."

Hearing this Herobrine chuckled to himself. Never in a million years would he ever had thought of being friends with a witch, especially after what one had done to him. But that was life in Minecraft, you never knew on waking up what the day was going to give you. Herobrine stood up and pulled out his sword.

"I take it you're not leaving then?" the witch asked watching as Herobrine checked the sharpness of his sword. Herobrine nodded.

"Good. Now thrown that toy sword away. If we're going to do this, you'll need to be equipped for the job," the witch said with a grin.

*****

"So how does it fit?" Herobrine moved his arms and then taking out his sword, he swung it a few times. It felt weird having armor on him again, but surprisingly it was snug and didn't affect his sword swing. The helmet was another matter. That was something he'd have to get used to.

You look the part," the witch said and pulled Herobrine's hand away from his helmet. "And leave that thing alone. I know you've never had one before, but you'll get used to it. I had to close up the face of it to cover those eyes of your's. To everyone you'll look just like any other bad-ass samurai. But you'll still have your powers underneath. Well, sort of…"

Herobrine shrugged his shoulders at her last comment, as if to say what do you mean sort of. "The bad news is you can't teleport. Well you can, but unfortunately there's no skin in all of Minecraft that will allow you to do that. If you try you'll leave the skin behind and reappear back in your old Steve skin," the witch said chuckling. "You'll just need to walk everywhere. But it's not all bad, there's some good news too!"

Good news that's what he wanted to hear. He'd heard so much bad news he needed something good to brighten up his day.

"Speak!" the witch said with a grin.
Confused Herobrine reached for his sword again to write on the ground.

"No you fool, put that thing away. Say something!" the witch said grinning again.

"But, I," Herobrine said and then spun around to see who was behind him. They were his words, but he hadn't spoken them had he. "I can speak?"

"Yes, you can speak. It's a little something I added to the skin. As long as you're in your samurai skin you'll have the ability to speak. Well, we couldn't have you going in there writing on the ground all the time, could we?" the witch said chuckling. "It wouldn't be long before they knew there was something wrong with the new guy."

"So I can speak as long as I'm in this skin," Herobrine said still surprised that his words could be heard. "Maybe this skin isn't as bad as I thought it was going to be."

"That's not the best part," the witch said reaching into her inventory and pulling out a huge sword. "What samurai would look the part unless he had a samurai sword?" With a quick toss of her hand she threw it in Herobrine's direction. Catching the sword, Herobrine marveled at its size and weight. Holding it up to the sun he admired how it caught the light and shone. Testing it with a few swings Herobrine smiled at the whistling sound it made as it passed through the air. This sword made his old one look and feel prehistoric. "Well, like it?" the witch asked. "I have to tell you it's got the same essence as ChuckBone's sword. Anyone who comes in contact with it will suffer a mortal wound. Once killed they'll never respawn. Here, you'll also need these." Holding out her hand the witch offered Herobrine a variety of potion bottles. "I don't know how many you'll need but here's all I have."

"Thanks!" Herobrine said putting his new sword away and taking the bottles. "Swiftness, healing, invisibility, I think you've got most things covered."

"You're on your own now, I can't go with you. We witches can sense each other's presence and it would only be a matter of time before I was found out. I can't go any closer than this, I'm afraid. But if you need me, and only in an emergency, you can call me with this," the witch said putting a small device in Herobrine's hand. "I never thought I'd say this, but good luck. All our futures depend on your success." With that the witch teleported away leaving Herobrine alone.

Chapter 4

While having to walk everywhere was a pain in the butt, Herobrine was glad of the extra time it was giving him. Walking alone and testing out his new voice, he went over everything that had happened to him. He knew that his agreement with the witch for SparkleGirl's cure would take him to someplace he didn't want to go. But never in a million years did he ever think that he'd meet up with another version of himself. It was too crazy to think of. Surely people would have gotten sense after the destruction he'd caused. But then again probably not. He hoped she was wrong, and it was just a wild rumor, for everyone's sake. The last thing Minecraft needed was two Herobrine's running around in it.

Almost at the camp Herobrine paused and looked up at the full moon overhead. So far so good. Waiting until night time seemed to have paid off, and no one had spotted him yet. But he wasn't going to be alone for much longer. Looking back the way he came he could feel his hostile mob sense tingling. There were hostile mobs on the way and they were coming in fast. Almost on cue the camp came to life. Where once there was silence Herobrine could hear horn's being blown all over the place. "MOB'S, MOB'S, WE'RE UNDER ATTACK!" Looking to the camp, Herobrine spotted a lookout tower, with a player inside it waving his torch furiously. "Nice touch," Herobrine remarked to himself. He'd wrongly assumed that because she'd left him, the witch had gone back to where she'd came from. But it looked like she'd been busy too, creating a small army of mobs as a diversion for him. Although he knew he wouldn't need it, Herobrine took out his sword. He knew the hostile mobs coming his way wouldn't hurt him, but he'd have to fight them anyway. If the lookout had spotted the mobs, he also knew he was out here as well. The last thing he needed was giving himself away before he'd even started. Turning to face the oncoming mobs, Herobrine swung his sword in a figure eight pattern to loosen up his shoulder and wrist. Then he waited.

Staring into the darkness Herobrine noticed the first signs of movement. Skeletons. Leading the charge Herobrine could see a group of skeletons had a head start on the rest. "Sorry guys, any other time and I'd be glad to see you. But right now I have to put on a show," Herobrine said to himself. Not waiting for them to run past him, he ran at them. Herobrine marveled again at his new sword as it cut easily through a skeleton, killing it, before moving on to his next target. Swinging his sword left and right, he cut a path through the skeletons and waited for the next wave. Looking back over his shoulder he could see the now smaller group of skeletons were being taken care of by the samurai. Then hearing groans and hissing from in front he turned to find himself facing the slower of the hostile mobs, creepers and zombies.

Giving the zombies a miss, Herobrine ran to the creepers and started to attack them. It wasn't a fair fight. Now that they could sense who he was, the creepers didn't go into countdown mode but just let him cut them down. He hoped no one else noticed. "YOU TAKE THE LEFT AND I'LL TAKE THE RIGHT!" a voice called out from behind him. Herobrine turned and found the first of the samurai had caught up with him. "You take those zombies on and I'll fight these creepers here," the samurai called. Taking his order Herobrine gladly left the creepers and started to fight the zombies. Just as he hoped, once he left the creepers to the other samurai they now started to put up a fight.

Launching himself at the smaller group of zombies Herobrine finished them off easily. Like the creepers, they gave no fight and never tried to defend themselves. As he fought Herobrine felt sorry for what he was doing to them. After hearing the story the witch had told he could now see why they'd been put here. To outsiders they were an enemy, but to the mobs of Minecraft they were there for their protection.

"Well that was easy!" the samurai noted looking at all the hostile mobs Herobrine had killed. "You were lucky we came when we did, it looked like you were about to be swallowed up by that group." Walking over to Herobrine he held out his hand, "I'm SanJab45… and you are?" Dumbfounded for a moment Herobrine hadn't realized he hadn't come up with a name for himself.

"Em, its em… KinHero32," Herobrine replied, saying the first name that came into his head and hoping it sounded OK.

"So KinHero, how did you come to be out here on your own? I don't think I've ever seen you before?" SanJab asked.

"Yeah, my mistake. I… got lost getting here. Dumb mistake, I know. Thankfully a local villager pointed the way to your camp. And well here I am," Herobrine said hoping his excuse sounded plausible.

"We could do with more players like you, by the way that's a fine sword you have there," SanJab said looking at the sword in Herobrine's hand.

"Thank you it was my brothers. He was a well-known sword-smith in our village," Herobrine said looking at the blade.

"I'd like to meet him and maybe get a sword like that off him," SanJab said.

"You can't… he's dead," Herobrine said putting away his sword. "We had a run in with some witches in our area. I warned him not to go after them but… he wouldn't listen.

Whatever they did to him he never came home again. That's why I signed up. I wanted to make them pay for what they did to our family."

"Glad to have you on board," SanJab said. "Now come on and you can meet the rest of the players."

Walking alongside SanJab and hearing how they were making a difference to the players in the area, Herobrine could tell he was a good guy at heart. What he was about to do to SanJab and the other samurai now just got a little harder.

Chapter 5

"Everyone I'd like you to meet KinHero," SanJab said to the group of samurai.

"Who, I never heard of him?" another samurai asked. "In fact what was he doing out there on his own?"

Herobrine watched the faces in the crowd and felt for the handle of his sword, it looked like his cover was blown already.

"We can talk about that later WickLan, for now let's celebrate. We scored a big victory tonight and put away a lot of hostile mobs. That kind of talk can wait until later," SanJab said leading Herobrine over to a table and sitting down. "Sit down KinHero, I bet you could do with a good meal inside you after all that exercise out there," SanJab said. "Bonten bring our guest over some food."

"Here's to ridding this place of hostile mobs," SanJab said standing up and raising his glass. Then as if they had all rehearsed it, all the samurai stood and toasted their drinks. "To no more hostile mobs!" they cheered and emptied their glasses.

Waiting for SanJab to sit back down Herobrine asked. "Is it always like this?"

"Usually. The only good hostile mob is a dead one," SanJab said. "But you know all about that don't you. Losing your brother and everything."

"Yeah, I do. So what's your story SanJab? How come you signed up to be a samurai," Herobrine asked trying to get the subject off of himself.

"Me?" SanJab asked. "I think it's the same as everyone else here. Hostile mobs ruined my happiness in Minecraft. I lost someone I was very close to. We were so happy here, we built a home for ourselves and they took it all away from me. We were overrun one night, didn't see it coming. I tried my best, back then I wasn't as good a swordsman as I am now, and… they got me. When I respawned I found our home destroyed and she… she was gone. I searched Minecraft for months going back to her old spawn points and nothing. It was as she never existed. I don't know how they did it but it was some kind of dark magic I'd say. After wandering around in the wilderness for a while, I came across some samurai and then started my training. The rest is history. They built me up, showed me how to fight, and I've been doing it ever since. We're like a brotherhood, all of us. We may have been weaker on our own, but now together, we're unstoppable.

"To the samurai!" SanJab said standing up again and raising his glass in a toast.

"The samurai!" the players cheered back.

Sitting back down SanJab grinned. "We probably seem a rowdy lot to you KinHero?"

"Naw, not really. Our Sensei was more of the silent type," Herobrine said. "Strict as hell. You stepped out of line and you paid for it. But that's what made us the players they we are."

"At last here's the food," SanJab said as a group of players came into the room and started filling the table with food.

"Come on, tuck in. We've got training first thing in the morning. I've seen what you can do with a sword I wonder if you're as good with a bow," SanJab said grabbing a handful of meat and stuffing it in his mouth. "Maybe we can have a match?"

"Sounds good to me," Herobrine replied raising his glass and finishing it off in one go. "I think I'm going to like it around here."

Pushing away his empty plate Herobrine couldn't

shake the feeling that someone was watching him. At first he shook it off as being in strange surroundings, but the longer he spent at the table the stronger the feeling became. Trying not to make it obvious Herobrine dropped his fork on the floor and quickly scanned the players in the room. Then he saw WickLan had his full attention on him.

"So are you the leader around here, or are there others?" Herobrine asked turning his attention from WickLan to SanJab.

"No, at the moment it's just me. WickLan is second in command," SanJab said.

"I don't think he likes me?" Herobrine said. "Not with all the death stares he's giving me."

"Don't mind him, he's suspicious of everyone. He's a good leader and respected by the other players but he can be a hot head at times. Give him time and you'll get used to him," SanJab said.

Picking up his glass Herobrine couldn't resist winding up WickLan. Lifting it up, he nodded in WickLan's direction and gave a little toasting gesture. As he expected he got an unbroken stare in response. He'd now made his first enemy. But it wouldn't be the last. Looking around the room Herobrine knew he'd have a lot more enemies gunning for him after of all this was over.

*****

"Well there you go!" SanJab said stopping at a door and opening it. "It's going to be an early rise in the morning, we train at first light. That is unless those hostile mobs decide to make an appearance. But I doubt it. Talk to you in the morning." Chuckling to himself SanJab walked away and left Herobrine on his own.

Entering his new room Herobrine headed to his bed and made himself comfortable. Right now he didn't know what he was going to do next. SanJab hadn't mention any big plan's that involved creating a new Herobrine, but thinking it over why would he. He seemed to be a trusting player but even he wouldn't spill the beans to someone he'd never met before. No, this time he'd have to play a patient game. He'd have to fit in just like he was any other samurai and maybe, just maybe, he'd gain some trust in the camp. That was if he could keep everyone else on side and keep out of WickLan's way. Going through his inventory, Herobrine checked through his potions and made sure everything was still intact. Happy that he'd be able to cope with any emergency he paused when he heard a noise at the door.

"Quiet, let's see who this guy really is," a voice whispered before the door handle slowly turned.

Chapter 6

Although Herobrine knew WickLan was suspicious of him, he didn't think he'd move on him so soon. This was all he needed now, this idiot ruining his plan. Any other time Herobrine would have waited on the other side of the door with his sword ready but this wasn't the time. He didn't know how much support WickLan had, and if he took on a group of players now, he'd never get his hands on the witch behind it all. Putting the rest of the potion bottles away Herobrine took out his invisibility potion and gulped it down.

Standing in the corner of the room behind the door. Herobrine watched as four players entered and fanned out with their swords ready.

"Well, where is he? You said SanJab walked this way with him?"

"Shut up, he was here before. I knew SanJab should have questioned him more. Taking a complete stranger into our camp like that. Anyone could put on a samurai skin and come this way. Now you can see how weak we are having SanJab as leader of this group," WickLan said to the other samurai. "I told you before, if we don't move on SanJab soon we're all going to die because of his mistakes."

"But we can't," the first player replied. "If we kill SanJab we break everything we stand for. We're a brotherhood…"

"Yeah, and it's that thinking that going to get you killed," WickLan said. "Taking on the role of protecting villagers and weaker players from hostile mobs, is that what you signed up for? When I joined it was to kill every single one of those things once and for all, wipe them out. Not sitting around wasting my time on players who can't take care of themselves. Let them die if they're that weak. It's not as if we're going to get rich is it? No, if I was in charge we'd be making big money off the big players not off a couple of farmers and villagers. Is this what you agreed to?"

Looking around the group Herobrine could see one head nod, before then finally they all nodded in agreement.

"That's agreed then. We get SanJab and that stranger out of the way. And then we move where the money is," WickLan said with a grin.

"But what about our sensei?" another player asked. "Once word gets back that SanJab is dead, won't they send another leader to us?

"No. They've already made up their mind, they want him out of the way," WickLan said. "They're working on something big, really big. Something that could change all our lives once and for all. They know SanJab would never agree to it, so he's got to go. Now come on, let's get to bed. We can get our hands on that guy later."

Watching the door close Herobrine relaxed and took his hand off his sword handle. So WickLan was going to take SanJab's place as top dog. He'd only known SanJab a small while but he could tell that he was the right guy to be leading this group. His only problem, like WickLan had said, was he was too trusting. Too trusting of his own players. Checking that the hall was clear of any danger Herobrine went back to bed and lay there. Although he didn't want to close his eyes he knew he better get some sleep. He didn't think WickLan would be back tonight, and he also knew that if didn't sleep he'd be respawning miles away from here. That was if he got killed. Taking his sword out and laying it across his chest Herobrine smiled, he'd like to see someone try it.

*****

"Care for a bit of competition?" SanJab asked pointing to the target tied to a post. "Or are you afraid to be beaten in front of my men?" Grinning Herobrine reached into his inventory and pulled out his favorite bow. "You're on!" Gesturing with his hand he pointed for SanJab to take first shot.

"It's funny," SanJab said pulling back on his bow. "That most people think that samurai are just sword fighters. But if you go back to ancient times we were known for our archery instead."

Herobrine watched as SanJab let his finger go and launched his first arrow, hitting the bulls-eye.

"I've noticed the new players are more interested in swordplay than in learning to use their bow properly. What about you, what do you think?" SanJab asked moving off to one side and allowing Herobrine to take his position.

"I'm the same as you. Why wait for something to come up close before you kill it. I'd rather kill it..." Herobrine said letting his arrow go. "From a distance."

"A bulls-eye I'm impressed," SanJab remarked with a grin.

"So how are you liking our camp so far?" SanJab asked. "It's unusual for us to get a lone samurai coming here. We usually get them in groups of two or three," SanJab said standing in line with the target and letting his second arrow go.

"Just a small class I suppose?" Herobrine added, seeing SanJab's arrow hit the bull's-eye again. "Most of my class dropped out. The training was too hard, or it was too boring, or as you said 'why aren't we training with swords' and more and more players dropped out. Most players would like to call themselves samurai but they don't want to put the work in. Anyway when it came to the last day, it was just me and my Sensei." Moving over to replace SanJab, Herobrine stood on his mark, pulled back on his bow string and watched his arrow hit the bulls-eye beside SanJab's arrow. "And here I am!"

Moving aside to allow SanJab to take his next shot, Herobrine turned and saw WickLan and his friends watching with great interest. Next time I could be aiming at you, instead of this paper target, Herobrine thought staring back at WickLan. He hoped WickLan could read his mind.

Chapter 7

"Good work men!" SanJab exclaimed at the players coming in on horseback. "So how did it go?" Pulling up his horse, one of the samurai dismounted and walked over to him.

"We've got two more villages secured and under our control. Here," taking a purse out of his inventory he threw it to SanJab.

"Good work. Get those horses put away and I'll send word to Bonten to get some food ready," SanJab said. "Well, you ready to go on patrol?" SanJab asked turning to face Herobrine.

"Ready as I'll ever be," Herobrine replied taking hold of his horse's rein.

"You don't look too comfortable around horses?" SanJab asked seeing Herobrine's horse nervously pull away from him. Herobrine gripped the reins and tugged the horse strongly towards him. Seeing that his rider was a lot stronger than he was, the horse stood in place and snorted.

"I think we've come to an understanding. I don't like him and he doesn't like me," Herobrine said with a grin, getting his horse under control and throwing his leg over the saddle.

"It's about time you learned the ropes around here. We've got another village a day's ride away that need our help. Say they've come under attack from a lot of hostile mobs lately. They can't pay much but then we're not in it for the money," SanJab said. "Well I'm not, but I know there are others who wish we got paid more." Looking in the direction that SanJab nodded his head, he could see WickLan putting on his saddle.

"So why does he stay then, if he's not happy?"

Herobrine asked.

"WickLan?" SanJab asked. "He's lost more than most of us here. Lost his complete family to an attack some time back. He was only young then. Hostile mobs came through his village and took the place apart. He ran away and was found hiding in a hole in the ground. He doesn't talk about it much but he lost everyone he knew. Although he mightn't like the small money we make, his hatred of hostile mobs keeps him here. But I know he'd secretly love to take over this group and command it himself. But it'll never happen. He's good at what he does but he's too much of a hothead."

"Doesn't that make you nervous having someone like him around you?" Herobrine asked.

"Naw, he's a good samurai, but he's not an idiot. He'll follow his orders even though he doesn't like them," SanJab said. "Right men let's move out!"

Watching SanJab take the lead and his men follow behind. Herobrine couldn't help but wonder if SanJab would regret not keeping a closer eye on WickLan and his friends.

*****

"OK, here we are. What do you think? I know it's not as big as our last camp, but we're getting there. We finished off the portal last week and in a few day's time we'll have more samurai coming through from the other side. OK enough about that, we'll camp here for the night and be at the village by lunch tomorrow," SanJab said pulling his horse to a halt. "WickLan pick a group of players and set up a perimeter. It's going to be dark soon and we don't want any hostile mobs getting a jump on us." "You, and you KinHero, get these horses sorted for the night. Aikina, you're on meal duty. Prepare some of that meat we got today."

Making sure the fence posts were secure, and the horses had plenty of food. Herobrine then watched the group

at work and marveled how well organized they were.
In what seemed a little space of time, they had the horses
sorted, a secure perimeter set up, and the first smells of meal
time was on the evening breeze. Whatever feelings Herobrine
had for his new enemy, he had to give it to them, they loved
what they did and were good at it.

      Queuing up for his meal of cooked stew, Herobrine
went to find a seat and found himself sitting beside SanJab.
"So what do you think of the stew?" SanJab asked mopping
up the last drops of gravy with a piece of bread. "Better than
home cooking?"
      "I know an army travels on its stomach, but with
portions like this. I think I'll need to make a bigger suit of
armor!" Herobrine said with a chuckle.
      "Glad to hear it, I found if you feed your men well
they'll follow you anywhere," SanJab remarked. "Now after
you finish that off, you can I are going on first watch."

      Left on his own Herobrine used that time to watch
what WickLan was getting up to. Off to one side of camp with
the players he'd been with last night. Herobrine watched them
deep in discussion and once or twice noticed them nodding
his way. He wondered if tonight was the night they were
going to make a move on him. If it was him he'd do it now,
out in country and in the dark, it would be easy to kill a player
and say it was a hostile mob that did it. The only difference
was he was going to be ready for them.

      Now with his belly full and his energy level high,
Herobrine joined SanJab and they left to find their post. "OK, I
don't know how you were trained, but we do one hour on and
one hour off," SanJab said. "Then after four hours, two players
will come out to replace us. OK you're on first and I'll get
some sleep." Herobrine nodded and watched SanJab made
himself comfortable and quickly fell asleep. Taking his sword

and bow out and leaving them within arm's reach, Herobrine stared out into the darkness. Nothing. In truth without looking he could tell there was nothing out there. Using his hostile mob sense he reached into the dark and found nothing answering him. This was going to be a long and boring night. Lying back down in their dugout, Herobrine looked and found SanJab fast asleep. Like a good soldier he had trained himself to fall asleep on command and was making the most of the peace and quiet.

Looking up at the full moon Herobrine watched as the odd cloud blew across in front of it, making the night darker before brightening up again. Taking no chances he turned back to camp to see how it was doing. As a cloud cleared the light of the moon, he found several dark shapes that weren't there before. It looked like any threat tonight was going to come from camp and not from hostile mobs.

Chapter 8

Herobrine watched as the shadows, using the cover of darkness given by the clouds, moved closer to him. "You really want to do this now?" Herobrine whispered to himself. Looking back over his shoulder he turned to see SanJab still fast asleep. For a second he wondered what he should do next. Should he point out to SanJab the danger they were now in, or should he say nothing and make a move himself. Thinking it over he realized that nice as SanJab seemed, he still was an enemy. He'd take WickLan's side no matter what happened. If anything he was on his own here. Feeling for the handle of his sword, Herobrine wondered what WickLan's plan was. Did he plan on killing them both and blaming it on hostile mobs? But then that left another question unanswered, how was he going to stop them respawning. Did he have a sword or weapon like he now held? And if he did, that meant WickLan wasn't working alone.

Putting his sword away Herobrine knew it wasn't the right time to use it. If he killed WickLan here tonight he mightn't have a chance to get his hands on the witch. However much he didn't like WickLan, he'd just have to put that aside for now. His mission was to get his hands on the witch. Looking back at the still sleeping SanJab Herobrine climbed out of their bunker and made his way towards the samurai. Pausing for a second Herobrine again put out a call to any hostile mobs in the area. Nothing. I guess I'm on my own, Herobrine thought. Lying as close to the ground as possible, Herobrine took out his bow and loaded it with an arrow.

Although this wasn't something he'd ever tried before, he

thought he'd give it a go. Waiting until the next cloud had cleared the moon he used the light to pick out his first target and let his arrow go. With a satisfying grunt he could tell his target was down. Crawling to the right and staying as low as he could, he again loaded his bow and fired an arrow. Two down, three more to go.

Lying in place he heard a confused WickLan whisper out, "Did you hear something?" Now that Herobrine knew where WickLan was, he loaded his bow and concentrated on one of the other targets. He wanted WickLan to be the last one left alive and then he could have some fun with him. With a smirk knowing at the confusion this was going to cause WickLan, Herobrine released his next arrow and hit his target. "Two to go!" Herobrine said to himself.

Having too much fun, Herobrine forgot all about the players respawning back in camp until he heard one scream. "We're under attack, we're under attack!" "Damn!" Herobrine swore to himself. Angry that WickLan would escape any punishment for what he was doing. Herobrine turned around and started to make his way back to the bunker. Moving as quickly and quietly as he could, Herobrine took one last look behind him. As he'd expected he could see torches coming from camp and headed his way.

"Damn!" Herobrine swore again. This was going to be a close call. Reaching into his inventory Herobrine pulled out a swiftness potion and drank it quickly. Using his new swiftness he crawled the last distance as fast as he could before throwing himself into the bunker. Catching his breath and putting away his bow, Herobrine turned and found a sword at his throat.

"Want to tell me what you've been doing?" SanJab asked. "Get on your feet!"

By the time Herobrine was standing he found the rest of the

samurai had reached the bunker.

"I knew it!" WickLan said glaring at Herobrine. "See I told you SanJab," WickLan said pointing his finger. "You wouldn't listen to me. I told you he couldn't be trusted, but you wouldn't listen to me. Taking a complete stranger in here…"

"Shut up!" SanJab barked not taking his eyes off Herobrine. "So what do you have to say for yourself KinHero? Or whatever your name is?" Herobrine stood in silence wondered what he should do next. He knew SanJab wouldn't take his word over one of his own. Whatever he said it would fall on deaf ears.

"Nothing! You've got nothing to say for yourself?" SanJab asked.
"You wouldn't believe me, no matter what I told you," Herobrine replied. "Kill him!" a voice called from the group.

"That's not the way we do things around here," SanJab said lowering his sword. "That's not our code. We don't kill each other." "But he's not own of us, we don't know if he's even a samurai?" another voice spoke up.

"True, but he still wears the samurai skin. No, he'll be taken back and face judgment." Before another word was said Herobrine felt a potion being thrown on him and then everything slowed down. "Now tie him up before that slowness potion wears off," SanJab said.

Grabbed roughly and taken back to camp, Herobrine was taken to a makeshift shelter and tied to a post. "I'd like to see you escape out of that," a samurai sneered testing the knot on the rope. "But please try, I'd like nothing more than putting my sword through a traitor." Leaving Herobrine to stand guard at the door he turned one last time and smiled. "You mightn't want to talk right now, but that'll all change tomorrow. We'll find out who you are, one way or another."

Left on his own Herobrine tried to shake off the effects of the potion and pull free of his restraints. It was no use, he wasn't going anywhere. Not killing WickLan when he had the chance was probably one of the biggest mistakes he'd ever made. Only time would tell.

Chapter 9

"Wake up!" the samurai roared, throwing a bucket of water. Herobrine glared back but it was no use. It was impossible to intimidate anyone when your face was completely blackened out. He hoped his body language sent out that message. "Get on your feet!" Before he had a chance, Herobrine found himself dragged upright by two other samurai just before SanJab entered.

"Leave us!" SanJab barked to the samurai in the room.

"But..."

"What did I say?" SanJab snapped at the samurai. "If he tries anything, it'll be the last thing he ever did. Now go!" Herobrine watched as the players reluctantly left them alone and then turned to face SanJab. "You know I really thought I knew you," SanJab said pacing in front of Herobrine. "But that's not why I'm here. All last night this question kept jabbing at me and keeping me awake. How come you killed those three samurai and left me to sleep? You could have taken me out first and then the others, but you didn't. Why was that?"

"You wouldn't believe me if I told you," Herobrine replied sitting back down.

"Try me," SanJab answered. "You won't have time to talk later."

"You've got a few rotten apples in your group..."

"Wait, is this all about WickLan. I told you he was a hot head..."

"He's not only gunning for me, he wants your job too," Herobrine interrupted. "It would have been convenient having the two of us killed last night. He'd probably blame it on a hostile mob attack or say I'd turned on you. They he'd have this group to himself."

"He'd never, why would he?" SanJab asked stopping his pacing.

"Complaining about money, telling you he wasn't earning enough? That you should leave the weaker players to themselves and go after the bigger players with the cash. Sound familiar?" Herobrine said hoping he was getting through to him.

"How do you know all this?" SanJab asked stepping closer. "I know him far longer than you, so why should I trust you?"

"You don't have to, but if I were you I wouldn't turn my back on that guy," Herobrine added. "You got away last night, I don't think he'll fail the next time."

"He wouldn't dare. He knows I have the command of this group. If he tried anything he'd lose."

"Care to put that to the test SanJab?"

"He'd never get away with it. And anyway why would he bother. He couldn't kill me I'd only respawn back again," SanJab said.

"I have a good hunch you wouldn't," Herobrine replied. "I've seen weapons that can take a player out of this world for good."

"How?"

"Let's just say there's more to this world than you think," Herobrine said.

"You sound like you've seen some things you rather you didn't," SanJab said.

"Let's just say more than most. And I know where you were headed last night. On a one way ticket out of here," Herobrine said. Herobrine watched as SanJab thought things over then walked towards him with his sword drawn.

"This might be my biggest mistake but…"

"STOP HIM!" a voice screamed from behind SanJab. Herobrine watched as WickLan and his group entered the shelter.

"Restrain him," WickLan barked at one of his players. "You

saw that, didn't you. He was trying to free a prisoner. So are you two working together, trying to bring this group down?"

"Are you crazy?" SanJab said. "Put those swords away. All of you." SanJab stared in disbelief as the players ignored his order. "I said lower your weapons. WickLan take charge of your men and get them to lower their weapons."

"NO!" WickLan screamed. "We don't take orders from a traitor. Take him." "You going to use your fancy sword on him?"

"What?" WickLan turned to see Herobrine looking at him. "I said are you going to use your fancy sword on him? You know the one that gives a mortal wound," Herobrine asked.

"How do you know about that, who told him?" WickLan asked looking at his group.

"See," Herobrine said looking in SanJab's direction. "Still think I was trying to kill you." Herobrine watched as SanJab edged slowly sideways before breaking out into a sprint. Then with a slash of his sword Herobrine's restraints fell to the ground. "I thought you'd never do that," Herobrine said rubbing his wrists and then pulling out his sword. "I think that's a fairer fight. Don't you WickLan?"

"It doesn't matter neither of you are going to make it out of here," WickLan sneered.

"Don't you think the others will get suspicious when both of us go missing?" SanJab asked moving beside Herobrine.

"Don't worry we've been planning this for a while now," WickLan said. "Once you're dead we're running the samurais like it was supposed to be run. With you, and others like you out of the way, we're going to be the greatest players in all of Minecraft."

"Our Sensei, he's bound to know there's something wrong when I don't report back?" SanJab added.

"You don't know, do you?" WickLan said grinning. "There's been a lot of changes since the last time you've been back. Sensei Sakura isn't in charge anymore." Still grinning WickLan pulled his finger across his neck to show that the player was now dead.

Seeing this, SanJab lost all of his composure and charged angrily at WickLan with his sword drawn.

Chapter 10

Watching from behind, Herobrine had to admire SanJab.
Taking on five samurai was either courageous or complete
madness. Not allowing the other players to gain an advantage
over SanJab, Herobrine threw himself into the fight. In all his
time in Minecraft he'd never fought a samurai before, but the
same rule still applied, stay away from anything sharp.
Taking on his first enemy Herobrine took a quick glance at the
metal in his sword, diamond sword. It looked like WickLan
didn't trust anyone else with having a mortal sword.
Pretending to lunge to the left instead of the right Herobrine
tested his opponent. After fighting off a few attacking he
spotted his chance. Being a samurai was one thing, but he bet
this samurai hadn't been in as many battles as he had.
Stepping backwards, he led the samurai into thinking he was
afraid. Then when he caught his opponent off balance, he
struck, slashing him across the stomach. One down, four to
go.
Seeing what was happening WickLan's group broke in two,
and Herobrine found himself facing two players. "I'd like to
see you get through the two of us. You're going to die here,"
one player sneered and advanced. Hearing this Herobrine
grinned, while most people thought of a sword fight as being
a physical thing. There was also a mental side to it. If you
could break your opponents confidence with mind games,
you could give yourself an advantage in the fight. Again
pretending to be worried by facing two opponents, Herobrine
backed away and then sprang at them. With a quick deflection
and a swing of his sword, he left one samurai with an arm
missing. "By the way I don't know if you know this,"
Herobrine grinned pointing to his sword. "But you won't be
coming back anytime soon." With a look of absolute horror

the player looked from the sword to his missing arm and then fell over dead. "So want to join him?" Herobrine asked turning to his other opponent. He knew what the answer would be and wasn't surprised when the samurai ran off. Now free, Herobrine looked to see how SanJab was getting on. Even though he was a great swordsman he could see it would only be a matter of time before he was beaten. Defending himself from two competent swordsmen he was doing more defending than attacking. It would only take one mistake and WickLan would have an opening. Running to join SanJab, he again was disappointed that no one could see the expression on his face. Grinning, he saw WickLan's confidence drop a little and his body language change. He knew things weren't going his way anymore.

"Only two?" Herobrine said. "This shouldn't take too long SanJab." Taking on WickLan, he left SanJab to the other player. "So we finally meet," Herobrine said swinging his sword to loosen up his shoulder. "I've been waiting for this for a long time." Herobrine noticed a flicker of fear in WickLan's eyes. "Looking at this?" Herobrine said holding his sword up for WickLan to see it better. "You're not the only one to have one of those. Want to know what it's like to beaten for good?" Moving forward Herobrine watched as WickLan retreated. He wasn't a fool he knew that once beaten his plans would disappear with him. Then he made a break for it. Knowing that they wouldn't have more time, Herobrine joined SanJab in time to see him kill his opponent. "We better move fast, SanJab. You know WickLan is going to be back here with more samurai."

"Get to the portal, it's our only hope," SanJab said. "Damn him, he'll pay for this!"

"He's not been working on his own SanJab," Herobrine said. "I think you'll need to kill a lot more samurai before this is over."

Trying not to look suspicious Herobrine and SanJab made

their way to the portal. Thankfully, WickLan seemed to be busy drumming up support, and they met no opposition on the way. "You know we'll need to break this thing," Herobrine said standing in front of the portal. "WickLan's going to be hot on our heels once we go through. Plus we can't afford to let the others on the other side know what's happened."

"That's easier said than done," SanJab said. "Once we blow this thing up he's just going to build another one."

"Maybe not," Herobrine said pulling out his sword. "I'll need an enchanting table."

"You've got one of those swords, like WickLan, how?" SanJab said recognizing the metal in the sword.

"Long story, I'll tell you later, but we need an enchanting table," Herobrine said looking around him.

"I've got one over there, in that building, follow me," SanJab said running in its direction.

On reaching the doorway Herobrine heard WickLan's voice call out. "They're over there, surround that place." For a second Herobrine tensed up, until he realized WickLan's group were running in the wrong direction. Closing the door behind him he found SanJab pointing the way to his enchanting table. "Quick they're on to us, you'll need to be fast," SanJab said.

"I hope this works. Or this is a waste of a completely good sword," Herobrine sighed placing the sword on the table.

"You know I've never tried this before. So if this blows up in our faces don't say you weren't warned." Using the magic of the table Herobrine distilled the essence that gave the sword its power.

"What is that?" SanJab said fixated on the green glowing cube on the table.

"That's our way out of here," Herobrine said. "I just hope it combines to more than just swords. Watch the door and see if we've got a clear run to the portal."

"It looks clear from here," SanJab said. "But that'll change, you go ahead and I'll cause a distraction."

Keeping close to any building he could find, Herobrine made it to the portal without being discovered. That was the easy bit, the hard bit would be trying to get the green cube to combine with the portal. Using whatever he could find in his inventory. Herobrine combined a pressure plate with some Redstone and added it to a device with a piston. Looking at it he hoped it would work. The only problem was, he wouldn't be able to test it first. If it worked they'd be safe, but if it failed. Well, that wouldn't be worth thinking about. Waiting for SanJab to appear, Herobrine felt the ground suddenly shake from a huge explosion.

Chapter 11

"I think that should do the job," SanJab said crouching down beside Herobrine.

"You think. What was that anyway?" Herobrine asked with a grin.

"Let's just say, our supplies won't be of any use to anyone," SanJab said grinning back. "That should keep WickLan busy for a while. He'll be too busy trying to put out that fire that we won't be his number one priority. So how's our getaway going?"

Herobrine held up the small piston device with the glowing green cube inside. "We just have to hide this pressure plate near the entrance of the portal and that's it," Herobrine said hurrying through his explanation. He didn't have time to answer questions right now and truth be told, he didn't have all the answers either. Looking around one final time to check that the coast was clear, Herobrine nodded to SanJab to go through the portal. Now left on his own he dug a small hole, placed the pressure plate inside and then fixed his device to the portal. Seeing that everything looked OK, he took a few steps backwards before racing towards the portal. With a last second jump, he cleared the pressure plate and went into the shimmering pool of the portal.

*****

Shaking his head Herobrine tried to shake the disorientation from his head. "Give me teleportation anytime," Herobrine grumbled looking around him. Portals were a quick way to get around, but he was never a fan of them.

"What was that?" SanJab asked coming over to meet him.

"Aw nothing, just don't like portals," Herobrine said looking back at the portal with a grin. "But I won't be the only one."

"Yes, what did you do back there?" SanJab asked.

"Well all going well, once someone stands on that pressure plate, that'll trigger the device. Then once the green cube combines with the portal… let's just say whoever goes through that portal will be going on a one way trip. And it won't be to here," Herobrine said.

"We better get moving in case someone spots us and asks questions," SanJab said looking around. "I don't who we can trust anymore now that Sensei Sakura is dead."

"What's in all these chests?" Herobrine asked looking at the surrounding supplies.

"You name it and its here. This is the main supply room to our world. They usually send us stuff through once a week. I guess there's a supply going through in the next day or so," SanJab said looking at the vast quantities of chests in the room.

"So anything different?" Herobrine asked opening a chest. "I mean, see anything here that you don't normally get through. Any sign that things have changed on this side?"

"No, not really," SanJab said opening a chest. "Everything seems like normal."

"So why was WickLan making a move on your command now? I don't think it had anything to do with me arriving," Herobrine said. "So why now?"

"I don't know but only for you I wouldn't be around to ask that question," SanJab said. "I never thanked you for what you did back there. You saved my life."

"Forget it. I was saving my own at the time," Herobrine said. "Just wish I'd a chance to get my hands on WickLan, that's all."

"Next time he's yours…" "Who's there, WickLan is that you?"

"Looks like we're about to meet our welcoming committee," Herobrine said crouching down behind a group of chests.

Herobrine watched as SanJab found a hiding place also and then reached for his sword. It wasn't there. In the heat of

excitement he'd left it back on SanJab's enchanting table.
"Damn!" Herobrine whispered to himself.
"WickLan is that you? Is it done? Is he dead?" the voice called
out again. "I don't like it, there's only two people who have
permission to come through here, WickLan and San…"
Hearing his name called SanJab sprang into action.
"What is it with this guy and his temper?" Herobrine
grumbled, leaving his hiding place and pulling out his bow.
"It's like he wants to get himself killed."

Catching up on the action Herobrine found SanJab in the
middle of a fight with three samurai. Pulling his bow string
taut, Herobrine let his first arrow lose and killed one of the
samurai where he stood. Now that the element of surprise
was gone, one of the two remaining samurai left the battle
with SanJab and came to challenge him. Not knowing what to
do next Herobrine charged at the samurai as fast as he could.
Using the moment of confusion and momentum of his body,
Herobrine dropped to the ground, rolled and took out the legs
from under the samurai. Sending him crashing to the ground.
Then getting to his feet before the samurai could, he picked up
the dazed samurai's sword and used it on him. "Two done,
one to go!"

Turning to see how SanJab was doing, he found he had his
attacker under control and a sword at his throat. "Who sent
you here?" SanJab barked at the samurai at his feet. "I'm
warning you, I can make you talk. The longer you hold out,
the worse it's going to be for you."
"Forget it," Herobrine said. Although he took no satisfaction
in killing an unarmed player Herobrine stuck his sword in the
final samurai.
"I could have got him to talk," SanJab complained. "I just
needed more time."
"I had to do it. They're already on their way," Herobrine said.
Looking over at the entrance of the supply room, SanJab could

hear the commotion outside. "We better move, follow me." Taking Herobrine to the back of the supply room, SanJab pulled some chests out of the way revealing a hidden trapdoor in the floor. "Just something I used to use from time to time to cover my movements," SanJab said with a grin. "Never thought I'd need it for this though. Come on quickly."

Chapter 12

"OK it's clear," SanJab said leading the way out of the tunnel. "We'll be safe here, hardly anyone uses this place." Climbing the ladder and coming out, Herobrine found himself in another small store room. "Well that was easy, so what's next?"

Herobrine watched as SanJab was quiet for a moment and then suddenly his appearance changed. "Nice skin!" Herobrine said remarking at the new samurai skin SanJab had changed into. "It's my old one. In fact it's the first samurai skin I ever owned," SanJab said. "It should make getting around here a bit easier. You heard that guy, he thought I was dead. I don't know what's going on but things have changed around here."

"So what's next?" Herobrine asked.

"My uncle, he should know what's going on. His home's not far from here, he can give us some protection," SanJab said.

"Can he be trusted?"

"My uncle, come on, of course he can!"

"You sure? There's a lot of things happening around here that you should know about but don't," Herobrine said.

"Even your samurai want you dead."

Herobrine could see that SanJab was finding that last comment hard to take in. He could imagine how he would feel if the same thing happened to him. But he knew that this wasn't the worst news that SanJab was about to face. He still had to discover who KinHero was. Herobrine didn't know how he would react when he found out he'd brought their greatest enemy to his home. This was one moment he wasn't looking forward to. But for now he'd play along.

"No. My uncle, he'll know what to do!" SanJab said getting to his feet. "He'll help me get some samurai we can trust. Then we'll go back and make WickLan pay for what they've done." Not waiting for Herobrine to respond, SanJab headed to the door.

Going into the bright world outside the supply room, Herobrine stopped for a moment and took in the scene. "So this is what samurai town is like!" Herobrine said to himself. He didn't know what to expect but was impressed by the buildings that surrounded him. Like a Japanese village from long ago, all the homes had beautifully curved tiled roofs that were supported by large wooden posts. Moving down the street Herobrine admired the large sliding doors that some homes had, which lead the way to small gardens inside. "Are you coming or what?"
"Sorry!" Herobrine remarked to SanJab jogging to catch up with him. "It's beautiful here. Much better than the place I came from."
"Glad you like it," SanJab said. "You'll have more time to admire this place later. My uncle's home is up here, just around the corner."

Following SanJab, Herobrine found himself stopping in front of a huge home that was much larger than the surrounding ones. "Nice!" Herobrine remarked. "It's big enough anyway."
"Yeah, he's one of the original samurai who set up here. If it wasn't for him I don't think we would have grown as strong as we did." Herobrine watched as SanJab stood on a pressure plate that rang a bell inside. "I hope he's here."
"SanJab? But how, you're supposed to be... what are you doing here?" a large samurai said after pulling back the main sliding door. "Where are my manners, come in, come in."
"KinHero, this is my uncle MoriHatori," SanJab said pointing to his uncle. Following SanJab's uncle's response Herobrine bowed back as a hello.
"Come in, come in. Did anyone see you coming here?" MoriHatori said hurriedly escorting the two of them inside. "I

don't know if you know it, but there has been big changes since the last time you were here. Sit, sit." Walking over to a low wooden table Herobrine followed SanJab's lead and knelt down beside him.

"I know all about it," SanJab remarked. "I was almost killed twice today. First by some of my own troops and now when I came here. What's going on?"

"Really? I'm shocked!" MoriHatori said. "You must be hungry, let me get some food for you."

"Not now Uncle, we need to talk," SanJab protested. "Eating can come later."

"Nonsense, I've got some food I prepared earlier. You still like fish?" SanJab nodded. "Good let me get it, we can talk as we eat and hopefully get to the bottom of this," MoriHatori said leaving the room.

"Your uncle seems a bit excited," Herobrine said.

"It's been a long time since, we've seen each other. Our families had a falling out awhile back. I don't know what it was over. So it's been a while since we've seen each other," SanJab said. "That's probably what it is."

"Now there you go! I take it it's been a while since you've eaten," MoriHatori said returning to the room with selection of fish dishes. "Eat up, eat up, then we can talk." As they ate in silence, Herobrine wondered if he was getting any closer to his mission. So far no had made mention of anything about a rogue witch helping the samurai out. Maybe this was the news that MoriHatori was going to break to SanJab.

"Uncle…" SanJab said with his mouth full of food. "This can't wait, what's going on?"

"It's been a long time hasn't it?" MoriHatori said gazing at SanJab. "You never found out why your father and I had a falling out, did you? He didn't want you to become a samurai. But after what you'd been through I knew it would be the best thing for you. I sent those samurai out to find you and bring you back. Since then I watched from a distance at how well you've been doing. I knew you'd be a good samurai but even I didn't think you'd command your own troop so quickly. You know in the early days this was all so easy, we'd ride out, kill a few hostile mobs and come back. But as time moved on and the number of players increased, so did the number of hostile mobs. We just can't compete anymore. We protect the odd pocket of players here and there… but we're losing the fight. I never thought we'd do this but we've turned to dark magic." Herobrine turned to see how SanJab reacted to that last comment. His eyes said it all.

Chapter 13

"You've done what!" SanJab exclaimed jumping to his feet. "All the time we've been trying to get those things out of here, and now you've joined up with them!"

"I knew you'd react like this," MoriHatori said. "Especially after what happened to you and your girlfriend. I knew you wouldn't take the news well. That's why we didn't tell you."

"WE didn't tell me, who is this we? Is this WickLan and the others, the ones that tried to kill me?" SanJab said putting his hand on his sword.

"I'm sorry, we knew we wouldn't have your support and well… it wasn't my decision but WickLan said he'd do it and…."

"You've broken our code, our brooootherhooood…"

Herobrine watched as SanJab started to sway for a few seconds before falling over. Confused he looked at MoriHatori and watched as his face started to go in and out of focus. They'd been drugged. Trying to get to his feet and reaching for his sword, Herobrine stumbled and fell over. The last thing he saw was group of samurai entering the room.

*****

"Ow my head!" SanJab said holding his hand to his head and looking around him. "You been awake long?"

"A few minutes before you," Herobrine replied. "And don't bother trying the door. I tested the cell door and walls, we're trapped in here good. Looks like some kind of magic at work.--I guess you were wrong about your uncle he couldn't be trusted. Here take this, it'll help to clear your head."

Catching the small potion bottle SanJab drank it down.

"Thanks, I can't believe it. He was my hero. Then he does this to me," SanJab said shaking his head in disbelief.

"Bad and all as he is, I think you're still alive right now because of him. Anyone else and we'd both be dead," Herobrine said.

"I can't believe it all those pledges and promises we samurai make and then they throw them all away. We swore we'd rid this place of hostile mobs and now we're working with them. I can't believe it," SanJab said.

"As he said, they've got desperate. And desperate people do desperate things," Herobrine said. "You've seen the way your men are starting to get stretched thin, it must be the same everywhere. Maybe that's the only thing they thought they could do?"

"You're taking this well? You don't seem bothered about us getting mixed up with hostile mobs," SanJab said. "In fact you never protested once about any of this? You knew about this didn't you? You came into my group, a complete stranger, and you knew more about this than I did. How?"

"You wouldn't believe me if I told you," Herobrine said. "I can't say."

"What do you mean you can't say? After all we've been through and you never once said, you know what, maybe all these players are trying to kill you because we're now working with witches and you wouldn't agree to that. I can't believe I can't even trust you!" "Got a little lovers tiff going?" Herobrine and SanJab turned to see a player look through the cell door. "Now, now, that's not the way I'd talk to Herobrine if I were you," the player said with a grin to SanJab. "Oh, you didn't know. That's why you're in this special cell right now. We couldn't have him teleporting out of here and causing havoc could we."

Without looking Herobrine could feel SanJab's eyes staring at him. Then turning just in time he found SanJab racing towards him with his eyes filled with hate. "YOU!" SanJab screamed landing his first punch. "You… murderer… all… those players… you killed!" Swatting off the blows, Herobrine let SanJab get his anger out of his system before seeing the player collapse on the ground exhausted. "Go on kill me then, that's probably what you've been wanting to do for a long time. Kill me!" SanJab said.

"I'm not here to kill you, never wanted to," Herobrine replied. "In fact I never knew you existed until a couple of days ago. You're not my target, I've got other fish to fry."

"The witch, the black magic, you're here for that?" SanJab asked.

Herobrine nodded his head. "It was probably her who gave away my identity. Probably seen straight through this skin. No, she's my main target. The samurai… I haven't made up my mind about you yet."

After he'd found out his true identity, SanJab moved to the furthest corner and stayed there without saying anything more. Herobrine look over at him, he looked a broken man. His whole world and everything he believed in had come crashing down around him. "I don't get you?" SanJab said breaking the long silence. "All the stories I heard about you, the destruction, the deaths and yet… you helped me when I'd no one."

"That's me all over," Herobrine said looking at the far wall. "The killer and the peacemaker. Some days I don't know which way I'm going to go. But no matter what I choose I always seem to make enemies."

"But this witch, why kill her if she's one of… yours," SanJab said. "I thought you lot always looked out for each other."

"I could say the same for you," Herobrine replied. "You lot seem to want each other dead too?"

"So why kill her? Is it because she's working on our side? Afraid she's giving away too many secrets?" SanJab sneered.

"You could say that. That and another one of her experiments that I want stopped," Herobrine said.

"What's that, a way to kill all of you in one swoop. Maybe I was wrong about them working with a witch," SanJab said.

"Maybe dabbling in the dark arts might give us what we're

looking for."

"There's dabbling, and then there's, dabbling," Herobrine said. "I don't think even you would want it to go this far."

"Why what's that?" SanJab asked now curious.

"She plans to build another version of me," Herobrine said.

Chapter 14

"Idiots!" SanJab cried out. "How could they be so stupid? Don't they know what could happen, the chaos, what if they can't control it?"

"Tell me about it, I was there," Herobrine said. "I know what I did and am capable of. But someone else, I don't know. She could create a monster a lot worse than me."

"So why aren't you out there finishing her off instead of stuck in here with me?" SanJab said his anger growing. "Surely you could just smash your way out of here."

"Believe me, if I could I would. I can't teleport out of here, I think you're mistaking me for the Incredible Hulk," Herobrine said.

"So how do we get out of here?" SanJab said.

"We! We're a team all of a sudden. A few minutes ago I was the greatest curse that ever lived and you wanted me dead," Herobrine said.

"I still hate you for what you did to us, but I can put that aside for now. Right now we want the same thing, the witch dead. Then once this is over… things are back to normal," SanJab said.

"What help could you give me? You're as big an enemy here as I am," Herobrine said with a grin.

"So what are we going to do then?" SanJab said looking deflated. "We're wasting time in here and who knows what she's doing out there."

"There is one thing," Herobrine said reaching into his inventory, but you're not going to like.

Holding the small device in his hand, Herobrine looked it over to see it wasn't damaged. "What is that?" SanJab asked staring at the device.

"Truthfully I don't know, I didn't get an instruction booklet with it," Herobrine said pressing and pushing on anything that looked like a button or switch. "I think that's it!" Where once the cube was a dull grey color suddenly it started to glow orange. Not knowing what it was going to happen next, he quickly placed it on the ground and stepped back from it. "I was wondering when you'd call me?" a voice spoke from the cube.

"What the?" SanJab said hearing the voice.

"Quick watch the doorway, make sure we're alone," Herobrine said pointing to the door. Getting a thumbs up signal from SanJab, Herobrine turned his attention back to the cube and spoke to it.

"I'm in a bit of a squeeze at the moment, but it looks like the rumor is true. There is a witch working with the samurai. I'll need help, the quicker the better."

"Who was that in the background, are you not alone?" the witch asked.

"Let's just say I'm not the only one who wants this witch dead. So quicker you get here, the better," Herobrine replied.

"Me? I'm not going there. I said I'd help you, but the last place I'm going is there. I'd be cut down in a second with all those samurais running around. No, you're on your own Herobrine," the witch replied.

"So what about that help you were giving me?" Herobrine asked. "Was that a lie?"

"Me, lie, never! I'm sending help your way, they should be arriving soon. You'll know what to do with them. Just make sure she doesn't escape, the last thing we need is her setting up somewhere else. Find her and kill her!" As quickly as the cube came to life it dead.

"Not much of a talker is she? I take it that was a witch you were talking to," SanJab said looking at the cube. "So this help she said was coming, what was it?"

"Oh I've an idea what it is. We'll just have to sit tight and wait. But when it comes you'll know about it," Herobrine said with a large grin.

Lying on the floor of his cell Herobrine looked up at the ceiling overhead and wondered what time it was outside. They had met up with SanJab's uncle at around lunchtime and probably slept for a while to overcome being drugged, so darkness couldn't be far away. He knew his support wouldn't be here until then. Calming his mind Herobrine sent out a message to any hostile mobs in the area and gave them his location. As yet he couldn't feel anything, but hoped that the cell wasn't blocking his transmissions. "It's funny!"

"What's funny?" Herobrine asked sitting up and looking over at SanJab.

"All the times I fantasized about meeting you and killing you. And yet here I am depending on you to save me," SanJab said. "Sometimes we used to sit around after training and plan out how we'd kill you. One player said he wanted to kill you, bring you back from the dead, and then kill you over and over again. Another one said he wanted your eyes as a souvenir. Another hoped you had family and he'd track them down and then do what you did to his family."

"And people call me bloodthirsty," Herobrine said. "I think there's some people in here who are a lot more twisted than I ever was."

"But now that I've met you…"

"You're disappointed? I'm not the monster you expected? You'd be surprised how many think that after meeting me," Herobrine said.

"Well yes, all those tales and rumors I was expecting…"

"Someone spitting out flames? Laser's coming out of my eyes? Cutting down every player I met? That's my biggest problem I've got a reputation that's far worse than I am. And now everyone wants a part of me because of it. Can you imagine living a life like that? Trying to find somewhere peaceful to live and then finding some player at your front door looking to kill you? It gets tiring very quickly. I know I brought some of this on me after some of the things I did in my early life. But what most people don't know is I was once like you, a normal player who just wanted to have fun here. That was until a witch took it into her mind that I should become more than I was and turned me into a monster. You think you hate hostile mobs SanJab, you've got a long way to go before you could ever hate hostile mobs as much I do. But you want to know the funniest part?" Herobrine said

"Er yeah," SanJab said feeling a little ashamed of himself.

"As much as I hate them for what they did to me, they accept me for who I am. Plus they're the ones who are going to get you out of this place!" Herobrine said. With that a huge horn started to blow outside. "Now if you'll get away from that wall you're lying against, it's going to be blown open up in three, two..."

Running for his life SanJab dived for cover just before the wall exploded.

"Thanks guys!" Herobrine said to the newly formed hole in the wall. "Now come with me if you want to live."

Chapter 15

Leaving through the hole in the wall, SanJab looked on at the mayhem that was happening in front to him. Although it looked like it was the middle of night, no one seemed to be asleep. "You control all of these?" SanJab asked pointing to the hostile mobs that were in battle with the samurai.

"Yeah, I know some are a bit on the ugly side and don't have much brain power, but I can get them to do most things. Now we don't have much time. Where could she be, the witch, where could she be?" Herobrine asked.

"You know I'm the last to know anything around here," SanJab replied.

"But if you had to guess where could she be?" Herobrine asked getting impatient. "These hostile mobs aren't going to keep this lot busy for long."

"If my uncle knows about them then it must be the older samurai who are in on this. Over there," SanJab said pointing to a large building on a hillside. "That's where they meet."

"I don't like ruining a good skin like this, but I've got no choice, we've no time," Herobrine complained. "You think you can transform, prepare yourself. And by the way I can't speak." Before SanJab had a chance to react to what Herobrine had said, there was a flash and the samurai skin fell to the ground.

"What the…" SanJab muttered to himself and then turned to see Herobrine in his original skin with his eyes blazing white. "Wow, I'd forgotten what you looked like!"

Holding out his hand Herobrine beckoned SanJab to take hold of it. "Oh yeah, I forgot you can't speak," SanJab said nervously taking hold of his hand. Before he had a chance to say anything more Herobrine teleported them away.

"Seriously that's the way you travel?" SanJab said shaking his head. "I think I left half of my stomach back there." Herobrine gestured that they were short on time. "Sorry, yeah this way," SanJab said running up to a huge Japanese style building and pulling back its door. "I don't know if they'll be inside but there's bound to be someone that can tell us what's happening around here." Once in Herobrine looked at all the samurai skins that hung on the walls and then spied the swords. "You can't take one of those, they're antiques!" SanJab protested when he saw Herobrine reach for a sword on a wall. With a glare that said he didn't care, Herobrine pulled if off and took it, then he took the one that was beside it as well. The last thing he cared about right now was how the samurai would feel about it. Now with a large samurai sword in his hand Herobrine motioned for SanJab to get moving. He knew the hostile wouldn't put up much of a fight without him. Once they followed their natural predictive movements it was easy to kill them. Herobrine felt a tinge of guilt for letting them get slaughtered like this, but they were a diversion and nothing more. He just needed enough time to get to the witch.

"Nothing!" SanJab grumbled. "I'm sorry Herobrine, I thought this was where we'd find them." Going outside they looked down at the samurai town below them and could see some fires lighting up the night sky. "Looks like they're putting up a good fight," SanJab remarked. "I feel guilty being up here and not helping. More innocent samurai being killed by hostile mobs." Herobrine glared at SanJab with his eyebrows raised as if to say, really? "You know what I mean, this isn't going to do anything to bring peace to this world. Once word gets around about this attack they'll be more players signing up to join us. It a vicious circle that'll never stop grow…" SanJab turned and found Herobrine with a finger to his lips. "Don't want to hear this?" SanJab asked. Herobrine held up his hand to be quiet. Staying quiet SanJab heard what Herobrine was listening to.

"It looks like the village is back under our control again. Just a bit of mopping up and they're dealt with. Any sign of that Herobrine or MoriHatori's nephew?" "None yet Sensei. But as long as we can protect everything down below we'll be OK. You can bet that's why Herobrine's here. The last thing they'll want is a witch on our side," the second player said and laughed. "So do we have enough samurai down there?" "Plenty, we've got the best on guard. They'll never get anywhere near her."

Herobrine and SanJab watched as the two players walked to a small outbuilding and never came out. "You think that's the way in?" SanJab asked pointing. Herobrine nodded. Reaching into his inventory Herobrine pulled out three potion bottles and handed them to SanJab. "Swiftness, health and invisibility? I suppose it can't do any harm," SanJab said putting them in his inventory. Waiting for Herobrine to finish what he was doing SanJab asked, "You know that entry is going to be guarded…" Without preparing him Herobrine grabbed SanJab's hand and teleported away. He knew a faster route underground.

Chapter 16

"That's the last time we do this!" SanJab protested as he realized what had happened to him. "It wasn't fun the first time." Getting over his disorientation, SanJab took in their surroundings. "My, someone's been busy! How far underground to you think we are?" Hearing a noise from behind him SanJab realized the two players that they'd heard earlier were behind them in the tunnel. Before he could say anything, Herobrine grabbed him and pulled him behind some rocks out of sight. Holding his breath for fear of being caught SanJab watched as the two samurai walked past them and continued on their way.

"We bypassed them?" SanJab whispered looking after the two players.

Herobrine nodded and waiting until the players had gone a far enough distance away moved out from behind his hiding place.

"You got any support down here?" SanJab asked, "I mean it looks like a lot of work has gone into this place. I doubt if we can just walk up to her and take her?"

Herobrine took a moment to still his mind. Using his hostile mob sense he call out but got a very faint sense in return. It looked like they were on their own again. Herobrine shook his head.

"I guess it's just you and me then? God, if anyone ever said I'd be teaming up with you, I'd say they were beyond crazy. I still can't believe it."

Herobrine smiled and then pointed from himself to SanJab.

"Yeah, I suppose it cuts both way. You never thought you'd be here with me taking down a witch. Is it like this all the time with you?" SanJab asked.

Herobrine help up his hand and did a horizontal wobble

motion that signaled, sometimes.

"And I thought I lived an exciting life. It pales compared to your's."

Seeing that the two players had disappeared, Herobrine signaled that they didn't have much time and they'd need to keep moving.

Following behind the two players Herobrine could feel they were going deeper and deeper underground. Whoever has set this plan up definitely didn't want anyone to know about it, not even the samurai. Holding tightly to the handle of his new sword Herobrine felt his impatience grow. He'd fought no one so far and he was itching for a fight. Anything was better than sneaking around like this. Watching as the two samurai ahead rounded a corner, Herobrine heard more voices. "Everything secure, you've had no trouble with mobs?" "Nothing yet Sensei we'd heard the village was under attack but nothing as yet. How are we doing up there?" "Don't worry about them, they can handle it. You three keep an eye out for Herobrine and MoriHatori's nephew, and don't let anyone get by you!" Hearing this Herobrine pulled his sword out and glanced at SanJab. SanJab nodded back in response, he had the same idea also. Holding up his hand as a hold signal, Herobrine counted down from ten in his head. Then reaching zero he grabbed SanJab's free hand, and they disappeared.

Being used to teleporting into fights, Herobrine had an advantage over SanJab and had his first samurai killed before he had a chance to react. Now taking on his second one he could see SanJab was up to speed had his player disarmed and was killing him. Seeing what was happening the third samurai realized he was going to lose and ran for it. Taking no chances and not in the mood for a chase Herobrine teleported in front of the fleeing player and let him run into his sword. "That's something you don't see every day," SanJab said catching up with Herobrine and watching as the player fell to the ground. "That's the first time I ever saw anyone killing a player like that before. So which way do we go?" Looking about him Herobrine noticed that the tunnel ahead branched off into two. "So is it the left one, or the right one?" SanJab asked. Herobrine looked at the tunnels ahead and remembered what Emman used to say, 'If in doubt always choose the tunnel that goes down.' Herobrine looked at the two tunnels and pointed at the one on the right. "Right it is then, let's hope you're right!"

It didn't take long to see that Emman's rule was working out for them. After going a short distance they came to a place that was unlike anything Herobrine had ever seen before. "What is this place?" SanJab asked looking through a large pane of glass. "You'd think we were in a zoo or something." Herobrine looked at the holding cells and didn't like what he saw, or more importantly didn't see. "So what do you think was in these rooms?" SanJab asked looking into another window. "Animals? Players? Oh God you better see this!" Running to join SanJab at the window Herobrine saw something move in the background. "Did you see that?" Herobrine shook his head. "I don't know what it was but there's something in there!"

Pressing his face up to the glass Herobrine used his glowing eyes to light up the cell. With a howl unlike anything Herobrine had ever heard, the shadow suddenly moved from a back corner of the cell and charged towards the glass. On instinct and to protect himself, Herobrine leapt back from the window, with his sword ready and watched as the creature bounced off the glass. "You saw that didn't you?" SanJab said shocked. "It had eyes the same as you, but it wasn't a player, I don't know what it was?" Herobrine nodded and then looked around at all the empty cells. It looked like they all had been occupied at one time. But where were they now? This was much, much worse than anything he or the witch could have imagined. "I think we're going to need more than these swords and few potions," SanJab remarked. Herobrine nodded, even if he could speak right now he didn't know what he would say.

To be continued…

Bonus Chapter From Herobrine

Revenge Of The Samurai

"You think its dead?" SanJab called through the glass. Herobrine turned and nodded his head. Putting away his sword Herobrine rolled the creature over and looked at it. It was like nothing he'd ever seen before. Covered with thick hair and made up of half player, half… who knew what, he wondered what it had originally started as. Was this a player who had been hideously transformed in a failed experiment, or was this beast made up of two species mixed together? Pulling back the mass of fur on its head, Herobrine could see its once white eyes was now dark. Whatever it was, thankfully it was now dead.

"You think you should really be doing that?" SanJab called out. "I mean we know nothing about those things, maybe it's just resting?" Herobrine waved the comment away with his hand and kept examining the beast. Looking it over he could see that it must have been one of the first experiment's the witch had done. Small compared to the room it was in, it looked like she'd started small and worked her way up in size. Opening the creatures mouth Herobrine examined its teeth and stared in horror at what he saw. Although small it was the ultimate killing machine. Reaching into its mouth, Herobrine carefully pulled at one of its front fangs tearing it out. Putting it to his nose he could smell the tell-tale sign. There was no mistaking it.
"Will you get away from that thing, come on we need to get out of here!" Herobrine knew SanJab was right, teleporting away he stood beside him on the other side of the glass.

"Well?" SanJab asked Herobrine with impatience. "What is it, what were you doing with that thing?" Herobrine handed the tooth over to SanJab. "A tooth?" SanJab remarked. "So?" Herobrine motioned for SanJab to hold it up to his nose. Sniffing it, Sonja's face grimaced at the stench. "Yeah I know, it smells horrible. So what?" Herobrine pointed from the tooth in SanJab's hand to his sword hilt. "You mean, you mean. No, it couldn't be. You're telling me it's got that stuff on it?" Herobrine nodded. "I'm glad that was a small one," SanJab said looking again at the creature in the cell. "So one bite and that thing would have given you a mortal wound? Wow. Thankfully it didn't have the ability to teleport out of there." Herobrine nodded in response, it had been this ability that had allowed him to kill the beast. Teleporting into the cell behind it, he'd easily plunged his sword into its back before it had a chance to respond. If it had had the same abilities as him, well, it wasn't worth thinking about.

"We better get out of here. I mean, I bet that witch of yours would want to know all about this. I take it she wasn't expecting something as bad as this?" SanJab asked. "I could tell by the look on your face that you weren't expecting this. You weren't were you? I mean, I wouldn't like to have thought you'd go willing in there if you'd known about all of this. Would you?" Herobrine shook his head in the negative. "Thank God for that. So what do we do next?" SanJab asked. Taking his sword out Herobrine pointed down the tunnel. "I thought you'd never ask!" SanJab said and grinned.

Taking the lead Herobrine lead the way through the twisting and descending tunnel. He didn't like it, going deeper into the ground wasn't a good sign. If they had kept the cells closer to the surface it meant that anything deeper down was even more secretive and probably more dangerous. "I have to give it to my uncle and the others, they kept this secret awfully well," SanJab said admiring the surrounding work. "I wonder how many know about this place. Other than a select few. And those… things. How were they going to explain them to the other samurai?" Herobrine held up his hand and put his finger up to his lips. They were nearly at the end of the tunnel.

Find Out What Happens Next In

Available in all online bookstores

Thanks For Purchasing Herobrine Rise Of The Samurai

Firstly I want to say a big thank you for purchasing this copy of Herobrine Rise Of The Samurai it's very much appreciated. If you enjoyed the book please take a moment now to leave a review on what you thought of the book. This not only helps me to write better books but also helps to get my books in front of more readers.

Keep tuned to my Facebook page and website below for details of the next thrilling instalment.
Thanks,
Barry.
https://www.facebook.com/BarrysMinecraftNovels
http://www.MinecraftNovels.com

CPSIA information can be obtained
at www.ICGtesting.com
Printed in the USA
LVHW021436020720
659584LV00025B/1312